Time Traveler's Limbo

C.H. Lyn

ALSO BY

The Old Tales
Song of the Deep

A Voice in the Tower

The Abredea Series
Hope and Lies

Truth and Fury

Miss Belle's Travel Guides
Lacey Goes to Tokyo

Damen Goes to Peru

Spooky Cat Stories
Spooky Cat

One Hell of a Road Trip

Spelling Disaster

Other Works
Love is Murder

War of the Unborn

Chapter One

Now

I picked today deliberately because this was the beginning of the best years of my life.

I sit in a café in central San Francisco. The sun shines through big, glass windows, warming my frail skin. My wrinkled, liver-spotted, and scarred hands clench the ceramic of my mug, the heat from my drink at odds with the chill in my bones.

I recall the barista, her flaming pink hair and the huge Star Wars tattoo along her shoulder. She was always nice. She's nice now, taking Roger's order and flashing him a quick smile before moving away to make the drink.

I inhale the steam from my coffee and down some of the rich liquid. I can only get flavor like this here—in the past. In *my* present, a good 30 years from the moment I'm sitting in, there is no good coffee. There's no bad coffee, either.

Roger gets his drink and moves toward the door. He's tall, with broad shoulders, dark skin, and brown eyes that glisten with flecks of gold in the right light. His smile brightens up the room.

I remind myself to look away. Don't stare so blatantly at someone who thinks I'm a stranger.

A door slams in the back of the shop. He turns his head—and runs smack into a woman wearing ridiculous purple heels. She stumbles sideways, and he reaches out to grab her arm. But he still has his coffee. Instead of holding her up, he spills his drink all over the floor. The woman regains her balance, and the two stand there for a moment, stunned.

"I knew these shoes were bad luck," the woman grumbles. It was a rough day for her. The numerous frustrations made this moment all the more special.

Roger blinks, looks down at her shoes, and cracks a smile. Then he meets her gaze and stares into those green eyes a few seconds too long. "Seems like good luck for me, though."

She flushes, and I do as well. Watching this unfold, I remember the heat rushing to my cheeks, the stirring in my gut as this man in this instant changed my world. That's me, by the way, the woman with box-blonde hair, green eyes, and a cascade of freckles across my too-pale skin.

She doesn't recognize me now, thirty years later with dark hair, weathered skin, and more than enough scars for the decades that have passed.

"Roger," Roger says, holding out the hand not dripping with coffee.

She gives the smallest shake of her head, like she can't believe this moment is happening. "Lucy." She glances at the coffee staining those ridiculous shoes and grins. "Should we get some paper towels?"

My previous self and the love of my life clean up the coffee. She's going to buy him a new one, settle the two of them at a corner table, and talk his ear off. He's going to love it. He'll listen with a wide smile, laugh at all the right moments, and fill her with an unexplainable warmth.

They'll get dinner the next night. And the night after. It's as if they can't stay away from each other. Now that they've met, it's like they have magnets on their souls, drawing them toward each other until, only six weeks from today, they move in together.

Their friends become friends. Their love for different hobbies, books, adventure, become shared. They build a life together.

Tears prickle at the corners of my eyes, and my hands tighten around the mug.

Let me back up, or rather, jump forward. In three years, the first time-travelers will make their presence known to the United States Government. They will warn us, and we will not listen. In six years, their warnings manifest.

In twelve, the face of the world is completely changed.

In twenty, most of the human population is dead.

In thirty, I'm the only one left.

Chapter Two

Now

At the twelve hour mark, my body is ripped from time and space and I'm propelled through a dark void. It seems to take longer each trip, but maybe I just like the dark. Maybe part of me hopes I'll get stuck here, in the liminal space where time doesn't exist.

But it doesn't happen. I appear, coughing and retching, doubled over with pain in the large metallic chamber coined The Blue Box. Not blue, not really a box, but it felt like a funny reference, and Rhika cracked a smile for the first time in months when she came up with it.

We were shocked the first time we laid eyes on the metal cylinder in Cheyenne Mountain. Now it's as familiar as my pillow.

I press a large red button on the wall, and the glass door slides open with a whoosh. I stumble out, my stomach still furious about my meal at the café, my heart aching at the sight of mine and Roger's first meeting, and my head pounding.

I'd stay. But I can't. Time jumps are twelve hours only.

If I knew how any of the technical bullshit works, I'd extend it. But maybe it's better that I don't know. The big fear when time travel was first created was getting stuck in the past.

That's a dream now.

I spend my morning going about the usual routine. I drink enough over-filtered water to calm my stomach. I check the radio, radar, satellites, even my little morse-code tapper. Nothing. Nothing for almost ten years now.

I tend to my garden; a few of the tomatoes are ripening. I'm giving the carrots another day or two before I pull one to see if they're big enough.

My collection of herbs used to make me wish I had time to cook. Basil overflows from planters in the corners of the vast green-house type space. Mint, rosemary, lavender, sage, thyme, and a handful of others I don't recognize. I've managed to keep most of the plants going.

It's hard to grow food down here, inside a mountain, but the military created this base to withstand nuclear Armageddon. It has sunlamps, water filtration, waste conversion, and generators to last a hundred people a hundred years.

Cheyenne Mountain will survive long after I've succumbed to age.

When I'm done with general clean-up and writing in my journal a bit so I don't go utterly mad, I sink onto the plush king-sized bed I found in the officer's quarters years ago. It takes a long while, but eventually, I fall asleep.

———— ◆ ————

I tried, you know. I haven't been wasting my time going back to snoop on my previous self. I haven't always used this miraculous technology to satisfy my own nostalgia.

There was a time when I jumped every day. Not everyone can do it; it takes a certain body and a certain mind. I don't know all the specifics, but when we finally made it here, they were excited to have another jumper. It was what got us into the mountain. The promise that I'd be another body they could use.

I'd jump. Twelve hours out, return, eat, sleep, plan. Jump again. Every twenty-four hour cycle, the same for days, months, years. It's hell on the body—worse on the mind.

I went years into the past, as far as the technology would let me, to try and convince humanity to stop devastating the world. To correct our mistakes, clean up the oceans, stop the toxic dumping, switch to renewable energy. I spoke to heads of state, religious leaders, billionaire moguls.

Some listened, some didn't, and most didn't care. Maybe it was a self-fulfilling prophecy. I came from a future where the world had ended, so nothing done in their time would stop it. Why not spend their money and enjoy their lives?

They didn't hear me when I told them how soon it would end. They didn't want to hear me.

Chapter Three

Before

Roger and I sit on the couch, snuggled together, enjoying our Sunday morning. My legs are lazily draped over his lap. Coffee drips into the pot on the counter, a bacon and spinach quiche is in the oven, and our friends will be here in an hour or so with pastries.

A quiet day. A peaceful day.

Until my lover turns on the news. I roll my eyes and shift away from him with a groan. "Why are you trying to bring the world's problems into our apartment today?"

"I'm just checking out what's going on." He raises a thick eyebrow at me as I move from the couch and cross to the kitchen. "Don't you want to know what's happening in the world?"

"No." I reach the faded pale green cabinets and pull down a set of mugs. The coffee maker beeps. I collect sugar from the jar on the counter, cream from the fridge, and get to work prepping our fresh mugs of bean juice. "It's all bad shit. It's always all bad shit."

Roger sighs and leans back into the couch, gaze on the screen.

"A litter of puppies was rescued from the turnpike yesterday in an act of community by a group of motorists who chose to be late to work rather than let these little guys get hurt."

"See." Roger gestures with one hand before reaching for the mug I hand him. "It's not all bad."

I glance at the screen in time to catch the next segment—an update about the war in Ukraine.

"Yeah, great." My tone is dry, and Roger sighs again before focusing on his coffee.

The news plays in the background as we get our oak wood table set for brunch. It takes up the most space in our little one-room apartment. Roger and Sam spent a whole weekend making it and getting it set up before Rhika, Nayaih, and I got home from a girl's trip.

The gift officially made our apartment the homebase for our little group. We have the most room to host, after all. They've been here nearly every Sunday since then.

Our three closest friends arrive within the next thirty minutes. We dig into our brunch, chatting over the sound of the television and planning our trips to the farmers' market, the park, and the antique store Rhika's father owns.

When the food is gone, Rhika and Sam take over the dishes. I stay with them in the kitchen, leaning a hip against the tile countertop, and talk wedding plans as they rinse and dry the plates.

The big day is still a ways off, but the happy couple talks about it every chance they get. I don't mind in the slightest. Sam's pale face flushes as Rhika mentions the first dance. He's nervous, despite him and Roger taking dance classes in secret to surprise her.

Rhika whips a towel at her fiancé, a smile splitting her lips. Her dark hair, touches of red lightening the nearly black color, is pinned back to keep the ends out of her face. "Stop worrying about it," she says. "I'm not planning any crazy choreography or anything."

Sam mumbles something about not wanting to step on her toes. She wraps her arms around his neck and whispers encouragement in his ear. They're almost the same height, his short muscular frame the opposite of her tall slender one. His cream-colored skin, splattered with freckles, and his short blond hair, is also a contrast to his golden brown bride-to-be.

I take over drying with a snort as he steals a kiss.

When the couple separates, we move on to a discussion of decorations.

"See," Roger cuts in just as we get to a conversation about napkin colors. "This is a funny one, Lucy."

I glance over, and he gestures for me to join him in front of the television.

I walk across the room with a skeptical expression, turning my attention to the screen. Beside me, Nayaih giggles with one hand over her mouth.

"A man has reportedly been detained after attempting to break into the White House. Witnesses at the scene tell us he was claiming to be a time traveler, sent to warn the sitting President about the end of the world."

I snort. "Yeah, okay. That's a good one."

Nayaih sombers after a moment, concern replacing her mirth. "I hope he gets help. It sounds like he's having some mental problems."

"Hey." Roger gives her a playful glare. "Don't turn this into a negative. I got in trouble for putting the news on, and I'm trying to make a point here."

Another round of laughter fills the apartment, and before long, we've shut off the TV and are heading out into the world for what promises to be a perfect Sunday afternoon.

It's hot for February. After a few minutes of walking, I tie my light zip-up sweater around my waist. San Francisco starts almost every day with a layer of morning fog. People complain about the cold; they don't like the chill that starts off each day. But I can't get enough of it.

I spent long enough in east Texas that the climate here in the bay is welcome every time I wake up to gray clouds.

Today the sweat makes my shirt stick to my lower back. I'm grumbling about it by the time we get to the farmers' market, much to the entertainment of my friends. Roger buys me an iced lemonade and my whining is silenced.

A few hours later, as we munch on hummus and veggie wraps in the park, Sam brings up wedding plans again. Roger's dark skin darkens further when he's officially asked to be the best man. His smile is ear to ear.

The blue sky overhead is clear. The sun beats down on us, tanning me and burning Sam. We decide to make the beach our main destination next Sunday.

My heart is full.

Chapter Four

Now

I don't eat in the morning. Not because there isn't enough food, but because the thought of forcing myself to down half an MRE packet with overly filtered water when I'm about to be in a place with real food, real caffeine, and real flavor, is excruciating.

I know better. Food from the past doesn't have the same effect on my body when I am pulled back to the present. I'll need to eat right when I get back—assuming I don't throw up for an hour.

But I've held off on jumping to this day, this time, for over a year now. I've waited, not so patiently, so damn the consequences. I'm doing this the way I want.

I materialize in a park in San Francisco. The grass is green, the rolling hills give a view of the bay—or they will when the fog burns off later this afternoon. For now, it's cold, and I zip up my jacket.

I get looks sometimes, for the tears and stains on my clothes and the triple-duct-taped shoes. This city has plenty of unhoused people, so I don't stand out too much, but I'm aware of the looks.

And I'm aware of the people. Every person that passes within twenty feet or so sends shoots of alarm through me. The same thing happened at the café, the diner before that, just about every jump I've made since I lost the others.

I shake my head, tears blurring my vision. That's not what today is about. Today is about Roger and past me. Naïve, innocent Lucy. The version of myself who hasn't yet learned how to filter water, how to skin a wild animal, how to kill.

Roger is here, at a picnic bench a ways away. He's struggling with the tape as he tries to string up some lavender decorations. Sam shakes his head and takes over the taping.

Roger wrings his hands together, dancing on the balls of his feet.

I didn't know he was this nervous.

My chest tightens as Rhika walks over from the parking lot. Her arms are loaded down with canvas bags, and she carries a massive tray of chocolate cupcakes with lavender frosting.

Roger hurries to help, taking the cupcake tray while she sets the bags on the bench with a grunt audible even from where I sit.

They chat for a moment, finish getting things set up, and then...

I remember my excitement. Nayaih was acting so suspicious. She'd called me up for a coffee date, but when we'd ordered our drinks and sat down across from one of our favorite parks, she'd fidgeted the whole time. Then, when I suggested we stretch our legs, she nearly knocked over my mug in her anxious flailing as she demanded we stay at the table for a while.

We joked about it for weeks afterward, how she was never allowed to be the distraction again.

She and young me walk down the concrete path, arm in arm, and Nayaih can't keep the smile from her face. Lucy's hand goes over her mouth as a laugh of disbelief breaks through. She knew there was a surprise of some kind. Thought it would be a cute date or the puppy we'd talked about getting, but this was beyond what she'd imagined. Beyond what I'd imagined.

Roger gets down on one knee.

Of course, she says yes.

I look down at the ring finger on my left hand. It is bare, the silver and amethyst engagement ring was traded for a hefty pack of supplies, back when people thought the world would go back to normal someday.

I might have kept the wedding ring if we'd had a wedding.

"Excuse me?"

I jerk back against the bench, hand flying toward my hip where—in my time—a blade is constantly at my side. I come up empty, as I always leave my weapons in the future.

"Oh, I'm sorry." Her voice is soft, a low rumble which pulls such uncontrollable nostalgia and longing from within me that tears burn in the corners of my eyes.

I glance up, my heart still beating fast as a drum. Nayaih stands a few feet away, one hand up in a placating gesture, the other holding a cupcake.

I forgot about this.

I glance behind her. The others are still at the table, chatting nonchalantly, but keeping an eye on their friend.

"What..." My voice is hoarse. I clear my throat and try again. "Yes?"

"Oh, I just wanted to see if..." Nayaih smiles, the fullness of her lips, the glistening white of her teeth, the kindness in her eyes–it's all I can do not to burst into tears. "We had an extra cupcake," she says.

At their picnic bench, the tray of cupcakes is half-full. I remember we ate the leftovers for almost a week. It's a kind excuse she came up with to offer something to a stranger.

She extends her hand, taking a cautious step forward. "Would you like one?"

I nod, my jaw clenched too tight to speak. Her smooth, dark hand brushes against my scarred skin and leaves a chocolate confectionary in my palm. With another smile she says, "Have a nice day!" and returns to their celebration.

My lips tremble. My chin quivers. I wait until she sits with the others, then I stand and walk away. I keep the cupcake. I'll eat it when I stop shaking.

Nayaih. The youngest of us. The kindest. The softest. The first of our group to die.

Chapter Five

Before

"I still don't know which is less believable," Rhika says, twisting her wedding ring as her voice shakes, "time travel or an extinction-level event."

Sam puts a hand on her shoulder and squeezes briefly before stepping past with his handful of portable water filters.

"We've seen plenty of movies about both." Nayaih counts again, pointing to each of the five heavy duty backpacks she picked up from the local hiking store on her way over. Five aren't enough to need double counting, but it's something she does when she gets nervous.

I don't tell her she could move on to something more helpful. I don't mind her counting.

In front of the television, Roger is on the floor rolling up sleeping bags as tight as they'll get.

"Those are movies, though," Sam murmurs. He puts a filter on each stack of goods laid out on the table. One for each of us. "This is real."

"That's why we're preparing." Roger stands, moving into the kitchen and putting an arm around my waist. The piles of food on the countertop, my assignment, are a bit pitiful. Food shortages have hit the city hard. We're trying to be smart. Get what we can and get out of the most populated areas.

Get away from the ocean.

Time travelers are on the news every day now. We call them Futures. They don't stay long. Every time they show up, they have a new set of information, but it's all the same. Earthquakes, tsunamis, arctic storms in the middle of summer, heat waves in the dead of winter, a list of disasters that—if they're correct—will wipe out most of the planet in the next few years.

I stare at the little plastic containers of dry rice on the counter, remembering that day, years ago, when we all laughed about a man claiming to be a time traveler attempting to break into the White House.

Where would we be now if they'd have let him in? If it hadn't taken so long for the Futures to be taken seriously?

"Did they say how many died in Europe?" Sam glances at Roger.

My fiancé shakes his head. "They aren't giving hard numbers, but it's in the millions."

Rhika and Nayaih suck in breaths at nearly the same time. Their eyes are wide with fear.

"We need to get inland," I say.

My friends nod, the silence of our apartment nearly suffocating. The tsunami that hit Europe was like nothing we'd ever seen. The water is still there, high enough to touch the middle of the Eiffel Tower in every image the news has plastered onto the screen in the last week.

Futures say it's just the start. They say to build ships. They say to build bunkers. They say we should have listened years ago, when all of this might have been prevented.

Less than an hour later, our little group piles into Roger's Jeep. We stay close. The streets are dangerous at night now. Fires are lit on almost every corner. Two days ago, a police car was flipped a few blocks away; it's still there as Roger takes us toward the highway.

Darkness surrounds us. The lights that normally make me worried about light pollution have largely been broken. Even the office and apartment buildings are startlingly dark. Occupied rooms are few and far between.

So many people are panicking. The highways are more congested than I've ever seen. Bumper to bumper traffic that smells of burned rubber and gasoline. Roger exits two miles and thirty minutes down the road. I pull a map from the glove box and click on my flashlight to attempt to guide him through the side streets and suburbs.

"Where to?" Rhika asks once we finally clear a fair amount of traffic.

I heave a sigh from the front, poring over the map and trying not to let my helplessness show on my face. "East. We know we need to go east. Beyond that... I'm not sure. Sam, do you have any ideas?"

Sam, the only one of our group with military experience, shrugs. "It wouldn't hurt to be near a base, but I'm not looking to be under military law unless things get real dire. For now, I say we get a few hundred miles away from the sea and go from there."

Roger nods, reaching a hand toward mine. "I say Wyoming. Basically no people, pretty far inland, and we might be able to find an empty cabin or something to hunker down until things get back to normal."

There are sounds of agreement from the back, and I squeeze his hand before letting him return to the steering wheel. It's a good plan.

My gaze goes to my engagement ring. The wedding is only six months out, assuming the venue, and San Francisco, are still standing. Assuming we have the gas to get back home after things calm down.

I think about a cabin and a slow smile crosses my lips. We could make that work. A little cabin wedding, just us and our friends.

Just until things get back to normal.

Chapter Six

Now

My normal day is short. I work the garden, hail the channels, make sure I have water for the next few weeks, and check the satellites to basically snoop on what's left of the world. I've spotted some polar bears near the arctic circle—which is a bit larger than it was a decade ago. It looks like outside is getting colder again, but at least it appears to be consistent, finally. There was a time the temperature would fluctuate between about 5 and 105 degrees in a matter of hours.

The young and old fell fast in those days. Anyone with trouble regulating body temperature struggled. Anyone without shelter when those cold nights hit... well, it wasn't only natural disasters thinning the population. Millions died from sheer exposure.

I read a lot. Cheyenne Mountain had some colonel back in the day who was obsessed with survival prepping, but not the normal kind. I had to pry open a nearly glued shut desk drawer, dig through a dozen keycards, and spend a full day waiting between attempting each one so the system didn't shut down, but eventually I made it through a door marked *Cultural Survival.*

Inside was a study, library, quiet room, call it what you want; the point is, it was full. Hundreds of books fill the shelves lined against each wall. They go up, too, the tops flush with the twelve-foot ceilings. There is one of those fancy roller ladders on each wall.

The center of the room has chests filled with puzzles, paint, canvas, those super nice colored pencils, and several dozen sketch books. I can't draw for shit; my right hand shakes from nerve damage a long time ago.

There are couches, a reclining chair long since faded from its original red color to an orangish mustard even though it's likely never seen sunlight. I spend a fair portion of the day here. Leaned back on one of the couches, feet propped on a chest, reading until my eyes hurt.

This room saved my life a long time ago. I found it a year after I lost the others, almost to the day. I was hoping to find medicine. Enough morphine to...

Anyway, besides my bedroom, this is the cleanest room in the mountain. I keep it well cared for.

After taking up a chunk of day with reading, I have some dinner, wipe down with a damp washcloth—zero water waste if I can help it, but I do shower every couple of weeks—and crawl under my blanket.

Pain eats up a few hours each night. Nightmares take a few more.

Normal days are short.

The days I jump, however, those are long. The tech takes me to the same time of day as when I leave, morning to morning, night to night, etc. Since I'm in the past for a full twelve hours when I go, I try to leave early in the morning.

When I get back from watching my own engagement, I throw up for nearly thirty minutes. Dry heaving follows for another thirty, and finally I'm able to chug down some water and it stays in me.

I don't have the energy for the garden, or the satellites, or food beyond a stack of saltines I put by my bed specifically for this inevitability. The first few are hard to get down. My mouth and throat are so dry. But I manage it, knowing how much worse I'll feel in the morning if I eat nothing tonight.

Seeing them isn't the hard part, right? I see them every time now. I go back about once every couple of weeks—my body can't handle more than that anymore—always to a date I remember. A time I know I'll be able to see Roger again, or one of the others.

Hell, sometimes I go to the movies just to sit a few rows back from them all.

No... the hard part is Nayaih. I remember it now, after experiencing it from the other side. I remember sitting with one of Roger's hands on my back, the other rubbing the ring on my finger like he couldn't quite believe he'd managed to put it there. I remember anxiety creeping in as Nayaih said she wanted to share some of the joy.

It's the strangest thing, remembering seeing myself sitting there on the bench. Remembering what we all thought was fear in the homeless woman's eyes as Nayaih spoke to her and handed her a cupcake. Nayaih had been a bit dejected when, a few moments later, the woman had walked away at a rather brisk pace.

How strange to know now that it was me.

Chapter Seven

Before

"**P**ut it down, please." My voice doesn't tremble. An oddity that I'll have time to think about later—if we get out of this.

A ragged man stands before me, finger twitching at the trigger of a cocked shot-gun. Roger is by my side, one hand clenched over a deep slash in his arm.

"You can't take these," the man says. His voice *does* shake. His gaze darts around the abandoned gas station convenience store. I can't tell if it's fear on his face, or frenzy. The gun jerks up, trained on my chest.

We only wanted to check for food, maybe find some clean water.

We're a few hours outside of Salt Lake City. The Jeep is still running, but the thing got busted up pretty bad trying to get through the city. We learned our lesson the hard way—no more highways, no more cities.

Since we got out, we've been going cross country. It's slow moving. Slower still since we've already used the spare tire. The trip to Wyoming is taking far longer than any of us planned. Walking might even be faster.

But we need the vehicle. Sunlight hours have started getting hot. Texas-in-July-on-steroids-hot. Having shade, a place to get out of the burning sun, has been a literal lifesaver. Nights are the same but reversed. Each morning we wake to spiderwebs of frost across the windshield. The cold wakes me up at night. We take turns with heating packs Nayaih brought. There are only six left.

"Keep it," I say. I glance at the crate next to the man. Six cases of bottled water, a Costco-sized thing of toilet paper, and thermal blankets. "We only stopped to see if the place was empty; clearly it's not. We can move on. No one needs to get hurt." *More hurt*, I growl internally.

Roger had barely reached for the top blanket when this man had jumped out from an aisle and slashed him across the arm with a long blade. The knife is on the floor now. Replaced with the shotgun while I was screaming and Roger was swearing.

"How many?" the stranger demands. His bloodshot eyes glance to the door.

Our friends are outside. Sam is trying to coax the last of the gas from the pump, and Rhika is trying to get ahold of her family on the phone.

The signals go in and out. We've gotten lucky twice. Long enough to know that my parents left their home in Texas, and to find out that Sam's brother is dead.

"Just us," Roger says.

I don't look away from the man as his gun moves, fixating on Roger now. His clothes are as dirty as ours. A vein bulges in his neck, just visible under a few days of scruffy black beard.

"You know where I am now."

I shake my head. "We don't want anything from you. We were on our way through and thought this place was abandoned."

He bites his lower lip, eyes wide. "You'll come back. I know you will."

"No." Hands out in a placating gesture, I inhale and let the breath out slowly. He does the same, unconsciously mimicking my pattern. Another breath, in and out, and his trembling eases, somewhat. "I give you my word. We won't come back."

"It gets so cold." His voice is quiet as he looks at the blankets. "Every night, so cold."

I nod. "Keep them. We'll go."

Curling my fingers around Roger's shirt, I tug, pulling him with me as I take a cautious step back. One foot, the other, a few paces with his gun still trained on us.

"Don't," his breath hitches, "don't come back."

I nod again. We take another step.

The bell above the door tinkles.

"Lu?" Nayaih's soft voice says behind me.

Fury flashes across the man's face. His mouth opens and time seems to slow. I lunge to the side, knocking Roger into an empty set of shelves as the blast goes off.

Chapter Eight

Before

Pain radiates down my arm, buckshot embedded in my flesh. I gasp for air as Nayaih's scream fills the room. I'm on one knee, Roger scrambling up from the ground beside me.

"Liars!" the man who shot me bellows. "Fucking liars, all of you."

He wheels the gun toward Nayaih. *No.*

I lunge. There is so much distance between us, but I did track in high school; I know how to move quickly from a low position. The gun goes off as I slam into his knees.

He careens backward. A bell tinkles again. There's a thud and a crack.

Then silence.

I'm on the ground, sucking in sharp breaths. Everything hurts. Warm blood drips from my left arm, staining the yellowing tile of this little convenience store. Using my right, I push up from the ground with a groan.

"Lu!"

In an instant, Roger is at my side. He grabs my shoulders and pulls me back. I yelp in pain; he releases me, staying close.

Running footsteps sound and I wheel around, terror pumping through my veins. Sam. Sam and Rhika and... a wave of relief hits so hard my knees buckle. Nayaih is all right. That second shot...

I thought...

The three of them stop short a few feet from us, their gazes going from my bloody arm to the ground.

The man is dead.

My gut churns. A metallic taste coats my tongue as the minimal breakfast from only a few hours ago threatens to come up.

His head is split. When he fell—when I pushed him—his skull landed on an upturned metal shelf. He stares, the same fury still etched in the lines on his dirty face, though his eyes are wide now. Unblinking.

"Hey." Roger runs his hand up and down my right arm, trying to meet my eyes. "It was an accident. You didn't mean to—"

I pull away. My back hits the low counter as tremors spread down my limbs. I clench my hands to stop them shaking. A red haze fills my vision. Sound seems to come through a long tunnel.

Rhika looks from me to the body, and then sets her jaw, takes the stack of thermal blankets, and walks them out the front door. Sam bends and picks up the gun.

Nayaih steps toward me. She puts delicate fingers on my arm. "If you hadn't done that, I'd be dead."

I blink a few times; my brow furrows as the words sink in. I meet her eye.

She gestures to the door where Rhika just exited. The top of the glass panel is fractured with spiderweb breaks. Buck shot has made a dozen holes in the stucco wall above the spot Nayaih had been standing when I slammed into the man.

The realization clears some of the haze. I lick my cracked and dry lips, then offer up a small nod. A few feet away, Roger watches me, eyes narrowed with concern.

"I'm alright," I say.

His nostrils flare as he exhales, that little movement enough for me to know that he knows I'm not being entirely honest.

"Guys." Rhika's high voice breaks the moment. "It's happening again."

Without a word, Roger darts to the door. I follow, cradling my left forearm to my chest. The individual pieces of shot ache and bleed. Some are deep, the metallic balls not visible when I glance at the Swiss cheese that is my pale skin. Others are just at the surface, probably easy enough to remove with tweezers.

Thoughts of my arm and the amount of time we will have to spend patching it up disappear as I reach the door.

It's a strange thing, these random fluctuations of temperature. We were caught in one just before we got into Salt Lake. Heat so intense the air rippled. Breathing hurt.

We found shelter that time. There was a cluster of trees at the edge of the lake. We parked the Jeep and stayed in the shade for most of the day. The water was the only thing that kept us going.

This is... different.

Chapter Nine

Before

Crystals dance in the air. The sky is clear, bright, and blue without a cloud in sight. Rhika, still holding the stack of thermal blankets, backs into the gas station store and the door swings shut.

"What is it?" Sam asks. He puts a hand on Rhika's arm and gently pulls his wife backward, away from the glass windows looking out onto the pumps and Roger's Jeep.

None of us answer. I squint, trying to make out the odd pieces of what looks like glitter coming toward us. I'm not good with distance, but whatever it is hasn't reached the Jeep yet.

Roger pushes the door open.

"Wait." I grab his shirt, fear clutching my chest.

"I want to move the Jeep," he says with a glance at me. "Get it right up against the window."

I swallow. "Be quick."

He nods.

In the span of two minutes, he angles the Jeep so the front door is right at the door of the shop.

In those two minutes the temperature has dropped maybe thirty degrees.

"It's ice," Rhika says. She puts a hand to the glass and a foggy imprint forms almost instantly.

I, and the others, follow her gaze while Roger hurries back inside with something in his hands. She's right. It's ice. The air itself is freezing.

In the distance, a wave of white overtakes the land. The grassy field past the gas pumps freezes over. Leaves and tree branches stop blowing in the wind.

"Everyone back. Now," Sam barks.

We follow his lead, pulling to the back of the store, past the body, and pushing the shelves together to create a barrier of sorts. We don't speak. Fear and pain knot in my gut. My left arm is useless at the moment.

"What do we do?" Nayaih's voice shakes. Her breath fogs before our eyes.

Numbing cold creeps toward us, drawing shivers and chattering teeth from the group.

"Here," Roger says. He kneels on the tile, hands fumbling with our portable lantern.

Sam darts beside him and pulls the matchbox from his hands. With a flick, flame is lit, and he turns the knob to increase the propane.

"Huddle together." Roger waves his hand.

I sit beside him, my butt cold on the tile, but warmth heating my face. He touches my shoulder before standing.

"Everyone sit. Rhika, blankets."

She hands them over without complaint and nestles in beside Sam. Nayaih settles next to her. Roger pulls a standing rack against the wall and drapes the thermal blankets to the top. They fall around us. He scurries in and pulls me close.

The five of us sit this way, huddled under a tent of blankets like children playing pretend.

The initial quiet after we've settled is drowned out by a horrible cracking. The sound whines and crunches, like walking on fresh-fallen dry snow. A shudder rips across my shoulders as I shoot a furrowed, questioning glance at Roger.

"It's the windows," he murmurs, drawing looks from our friends. "The cold, freezing the glass."

"Will the Jeep be okay?" Nayaih asks.

Roger shrugs one shoulder.

"It'll be okay." Sam's arm tightens around Rhika as she rests her head against his chest. "This will be like the heat wave. It will pass."

None of us question the certainty in his voice. None of us want to think of what will happen if he is wrong.

We fall into silence, listening to the ice crawling toward us. The temperature drops further. The exposed nerves in my arm send shoots of pain to my brain. It's like those little metal balls are frozen inside my flesh, though I doubt it's actually *that* cold.

I'll need to remove them, but that's not possible right now. Our medical supplies—if the first aid kit Sam grabbed from his kindergarten class on the way to our place just before we left San Francisco counts as medical supplies—are in the Jeep.

Deep inhales and slow exhales distract a little from the pain.

The heat from my fiancé warms the right side of my body. I press in closer, needing the warmth, but needing the comfort more.

Outside of our nest, a man lies dead.

I killed him.

Chapter Ten

Now

The world ended before I made it into this bunker. It ended before myself, my fiancé, and our friends got to what we had hoped would be a safe place.

Nowhere was safe. It took far too long for us to figure that out. To figure out that humanity wasn't worth fighting for at that point.

I get back from another trip to my past. Young Lucy and Roger went to lunch, preparing for the wedding. I remember it well. I remember the exact date because it was the first time my parents visited us in San Francisco.

We all got lunch at a café close to our apartment. Dad insisted on paying, but Roger's ploy for the check endeared him to my family. My mom spent the entire time worried about the seating arrangement, before we politely explained that we were keeping things small, not having a seating arrangement, and didn't plan on inviting anyone who would cause enough trouble to require assigned seating.

It struck me as surreal, yet again, seeing my parents. It's the first time I've seen them in thirty years. I look so much like my mom now. An older version of her, with more wrinkles, grayer hair, and a multitude of scars.

When I return from my trip down memory lane, I'm overcome. A combination of physical, mental, and emotional pain and exhaustion cling to me. I down a full glass of water before the retching takes hold, but I'm still doubled over, on my knees in front of the bucket I keep by the Blue Box for just such an occasion.

My vision blurs with tears. Heat pummels my face and chest.

I didn't think seeing them would hurt this much. I loved them. They were decent parents; of course I loved them. But we didn't see each other often. We were a holiday get-together kind of family, not the kind who called each other every week.

When it all went bad, when the world caught fire, and everyone went crazy and a man shot me in a convenience store right before I killed him...

I shake my head, stringy hair dangling in my face as I swallow down metallic tasting spit.

I wanted them back. I wanted my mom and dad at the end of the world.

I wanted to at least get to say goodbye.

My back aches. Sinking onto my heels, then leaning against the glass door to the time machine with my ass on the cold concrete, I stare at my shaking hands.

Something beeps.

Sucking in a breath, I struggle to my feet and follow the sound. Cheyenne Mountain is a military base. A lot of things beep. I learned long ago not to panic at the sound.

It's likely one of the satellites picked up interference somewhere. Or the radio caught an old channel with an emergency broadcast still going. There have been a few of them through the years.

The control room—as I call it—is wall to wall screens. Some show images from half a dozen satellites still in orbit. Some are black, the screens shut off because their cameras are inside the base, and I couldn't keep staring at empty hallways.

Two of them show the world just outside the mountain. Those are the ones I look at the most. They tell me what the weather is like. I've watched snow pile up to cover their lenses, seen it melt away a day later. I've watched winds rip trees up by the roots.

There used to be over a dozen of these cameras, going from the highway to the massive metal bunker door. These are right outside that door, partially hidden in the rock of the mountain.

They are the only two remaining.

Right now, they are lying to me.

Chapter Eleven

Now

A rigorous shake of my head only serves to make me dizzy. It doesn't get rid of the hallucination I'm seeing on the screens in front of me. I'm frozen, my mind stuck for several long seconds.

I stagger backward and sink into the patchy office chair. It's got holes in the cushion from me picking at it over the years. Years.

A decade.

Longer.

I do the math for the first time in a long time. The others died over twelve years ago. The radios all went silent a few months later. The satellites have shown nothing but ice and flame and destruction.

So how is it possible that three people are standing outside my bunker right now?

One of them is small. A child.

I shake my head again, pressing my fingers against my forehead. I did two jumps barely a week apart. That's what this is. Time sickness. Fatigue.

Not real. It's not real.

My heart beats at an irrational pace. Sweat beads at my hairline and the back of my neck. I push up from the chair, stride from the room, and follow the long gray hallway to the officer's quarters I claimed as my bedroom after the others died.

The air doesn't feel right here. The space is too wide. The blankets too soft.

I backtrack, making for the small dorm room Roger and I were assigned when we arrived here.

My footsteps echo down the long, stark hallway. I've avoided this path.

Two cots are pushed together against the far wall. It wasn't comfortable, but it wasn't sleeping outside. Better than nothing, that's what Roger said. Better than living in the elements.

But I was unsure. After everything we'd gone through, the distance, the loss, the death... this place seemed too good to be true.

I crawl under the scratchy blanket and thin sheet still on the bed. Blooms of dust float into the air, making me cough a few times.

They were happy to have me. Another person able to jump. Another Future. When the people running the base finally realized what I was capable of, they brought us in. Gave us shelter. Let us skip the lottery.

When we got inside, we realized the truth. There was no need for a lottery. No need for the people huddled in make-shift shelters outside.

Cheyenne Mountain was essentially empty. A dozen people were left, with room for hundreds.

Roger was horrified; Sam, too. I understood. They'd done the math. Figured out if they let everyone in, there would be problems. Theft, assaults, chaos; people would cause trouble. The remaining original members of the base would have to set up rationing, schedules. They'd have to make the mountain a place to live, not just a place to survive.

We spent almost a year here. Roger trying every day to convince them to bring in the other survivors. Every day, failing. It was too much for Sam. He was in the brig more often than not. I think it hurt his cause more than helped, making so much trouble all the time.

I don't know which of them it was, Roger or Sam. Maybe neither; maybe the general finally saw their side of things.

I was on a jump. They let someone in. One of the last people outside, or maybe the last—I never saw anyone on the cameras after that.

By the time I got back from the past, everyone in the mountain was dead. The stranger had slaughtered them, from what I could tell.

I found his body last, next to several empty bottles of liquor and about half the pharmacy of emergency meds.

That's what happened last time someone came into the mountain.

Chapter Twelve

Before

I run my fingers over the little bumps on my arm. Circular scars where Rhika picked out pieces of buckshot with tweezers a few weeks ago.

Roger's warm hand pulls my fingers from the scar tissue. He presses them to his lips. "Hey, you okay?"

He speaks in a low murmur to not wake the others.

We finally made it. Found a cabin in the middle of nowhere. Seedlings are growing on the windowsill, Sam caught a rabbit a few days ago, the weather has been consistent for days, and for the first time in a long time, it feels like we're going to get through this.

The quiet means my brain has time to think. Time to conjure up the image of the man I killed. His vacant eyes haunt my sleep. Even in a real bed, with Roger holding me through the night, I can't get more than a few hours in a row.

I nod against his shoulder. "I'll be okay."

"You're not now." He doesn't ask it. He's seen it in me since that day.

"No," I whisper. "Not really. Not yet. I keep..."

He squeezes me as my throat constricts.

"I keep seeing him in my dreams."

The scruff on his chin scratches my forehead. None of us have shaved in over a month. Who knew it would take him so long to grow a beard?

His breath caresses my skin. "I keep seeing you."

"What?"

He shifts, meeting my eyes for a brief moment before pulling me back into his chest. "I keep seeing you bleeding. When he shot you..."

His heartbeat quickens, the sound muffled against my ear.

I swallow. "I was worried he'd gotten Nayaih."

He nods. "Me too." He hesitates, his body tense. "I feel... I feel responsible for what happened. It's my fault you were hurt. My fault he fired at us."

I sit up, half of me hating it as I pull away from him. But I need to see his face for this discussion. I gaze into his dark eyes, hooded with guilt.

"It's not your fault, Roger."

He shakes his head, sitting up and picking at his fingers. "I lied about how many people we had. If I'd told the truth—"

"He'd have killed us then and there," I interrupt. "He was waiting for an excuse to shoot." The comforting words are for my lover, but they solidify something within me as well. "If we'd have left, we'd have died. We needed those blankets. If we'd been out in the cold?"

I take his hand, our fingers entwining.

"It still keeps me up."

I nod. "Me too." I nudge his shoulder with mine. "We'll definitely need therapy when this is over."

That brings out a hoarse laugh, and a smile flickers across my face. I've missed that laugh. It used to come so naturally.

We snuggle together, eventually falling into fitful sleep.

◆◇◆

Nayaih is sick.

Worry clenches my stomach each time she coughs. It's a gravely sound, wracking her frail body and sending Rhika scurrying over with warm water each time. Nothing seems to help.

It started a few days ago with a runny nose and a headache. She stayed in the little cabin, sleeping for hours while the rest of us went to find water and attempt hunting.

When we returned, her fever was dangerously high. Sweat soaks through each blanket we put around her. The effort to keep her hydrated is shared between the four of us, as well as the anxiety every time she shakes her head with a shiver and pushes the cup away.

Rhika is inside with her, holding a cold compress to her forehead. Sam, Roger, and I discuss our options in front of the Jeep.

"We need medicine."

The men nod.

Sam points to a spot on the map. "Even without knowing the exact spot, we're somewhere around here. Which means there's a town a few hours walk north. We should be able to find a pharmacy or something."

"We don't need much," Roger says. "Just something to bring down that damn fever."

"Getting some food wouldn't hurt." I glance at the string of rabbits bleeding from a tree a dozen yards away. "None of the crops we have will be ready to harvest for a long time, and that's assuming we don't get another heat wave that kills them all."

"That's my main concern." Roger taps his hand on the hood of the Jeep and glances toward the cabin. "A heat wave, or a cold spell, while we're out. We don't have any kind of warning."

Sam nods. "We'll have to pack enough to contend with whatever happens."

"Who's staying?" I cross my arms, torn between wanting to be here for Nayaih and knowing that I'm the next best shot after Sam. Roger hasn't quite gotten the hang of it, but I grew up in Texas.

"I think Rhika should stay." A flash of guilt crosses Sam's face. He wants to keep his wife safe, but we all know how she will respond to being left behind.

"Should you stay too?" I look to Roger.

His eyes widen before his brow furrows. He chews his bottom lip for a moment, frowning at me. "Do you want me to stay?"

I shake my head. "I don't want to leave Rhika alone with Nayaih. If something happens and she needs help? I just don't think any one of us should be left alone. If Nayaih was up and moving I'd say all three of us go, but it'll basically be Rhika by herself."

Sam looks from me to Roger. "I'll go tell Rhika the plan while you two get this sorted."

Roger nods as Sam claps a hand on his shoulder and heads back into the cabin.

I take my fiancé's hand, the ring on my finger glinting in the morning light. "I don't want to go without you, but Sam and I have the best chance of getting there and back quick."

"Take the Jeep."

My gaze darts to his face, analyzing the steel in his expression. "Are you sure?"

He grimaces, jaw clenched. "If it's just you and Sam I want you both back as soon as possible. There isn't much left, but there should be enough gas to get you there and back."

I squeeze his fingers. "We can try to fill up while we're in town."

Roger runs a hand across his forehead, the other squeezing me back. "Don't waste any time. Get in, find some medicine, and come back."

I nod.

Sam and I get ready and, before the sun has reached its highest point in the sky, we are rumbling down the dirt road toward the town ten miles away.

Chapter Thirteen

Before

The west coast is gone.

According to the news broadcast Sam is able to pick up on the Jeep's radio, everything a hundred miles in from the ocean is flooded. We exchange a look as the newscaster chokes back a sob. San Francisco was obliterated.

"I'm glad we left when we did," I murmur, tweaking the steering wheel to avoid a large dip in the road.

Sam doesn't speak, but I catch his nod in my peripheral vision. He turns up the volume, and we listen to endless lists of devastation. Tornadoes ripping across Canada. Fires consuming the midwest. No news from Europe in days.

"Reports of mass rioting and looting in every major city still standing have those of us left wondering if it's worth trying to find shelter."

I glance at the radio. The heartbreak in this woman's voice is piercing as I think of the man who shot me.

Sam punches the off button a little too hard, and we drive in silence. I slow once we reach a sign naming the town "Fair Weather." The irony is not lost on me. I roll my eyes as I pull to the side of the road.

"Park here and walk in?"

Sam agrees. We load up our packs. We've each brought a thermal blanket, fire starter, and full bottles of water. If the cold hits again we might have time to find shelter. If it's a heat wave... shade and staying hydrated are the most we can hope for.

We hike in, following the cracked asphalt of the road. The intense change in weather has already done significant damage. The trees on either side are baren. Bark is scorched with burn marks from where the heat hit too hard. The street itself is marred with pockets where ice slammed down from the sky. Any moisture in tiny cracks expanded with each freeze. Little lines in the road have become jagged slices across it.

Fair Weather has a population of 500. At least, it did when the sign was put up. I don't know what I'd prefer as we walk toward our destination : an untouched town where life has continued on as normal, or a ghost town.

"Enough people that they should have a pharmacy," Sam says as we pass the sign.

I nod. "Do you think we brought enough to trade?"

"Yeah, but I'm hoping we won't have to. I don't want to lose any of what we've got."

I nod again. "But for Nayaih—"

"Of course." He sighs and runs a hand through his shaggy hair. It's hard to keep that military cut during the end of the world. "But it wouldn't do us any good getting rid of all our water filters or fire starters."

"Agreed. Maybe there won't be anyone there."

"If they fled, we have to hope they didn't empty the meds first."

"If not?" I glance at him and hitch my backpack a little higher. Nerves tingle down the back of my spine. Anticipation stirs in my gut. "What if they don't want to trade? What if they won't give us the medicine."

Sam stops, and I take a step past him before I turn. He meets my gaze with hard blue eyes. Eyes that have seen war, seen the worst of what humanity has to offer. Eyes that filled with tears when he saw Rhika coming down the aisle, henna covering her hands and arms, her dress a stunning thing of red and gold.

We've been friends for years. Roger knew Sam before he joined the military. They grew up together. When I met him, he and Rhika were already engaged. It didn't take long for them to pull me fully into their little family, and

Nayaih too. The five of us have been nearly inseparable ever since.

I've seen Sam cry twice. Once at the wedding, then again when he and Rhika found out they'd never be able to have children of their own.

Roger went right to work that day. We got the call while they were still at the doctor's office, and Roger dove into research mode. He looked up unconventional medicine, adoption paperwork, foster care classes... all of it.

It's one of the things I love about him. He's a fixer.

But Sam and Rhika didn't need a fix in that moment. They needed their friends. They needed to grieve. So, while Roger called every adoption agency in the bay area, I picked up some food and took it to Sam and Rhika's apartment. I got their schedules cleared at work for a few days. I sat with them while they cried.

Sam blinks and my thoughts are pulled away from the past and back to the moment at hand. His gaze darts to the rifle slung across my shoulder. "If it comes to it, we do what we must to keep our family safe."

A chill runs down my spine. Then I think of the blast that nearly carved my best friend to pieces. The chill solidifies into something icy and hard in my chest.

I give Sam a solemn nod, and we continue on our way.

Chapter Fourteen

Now

I t doesn't make sense.

My first thought when I wake in the middle of what must be night—it's hard to tell down here, and I don't have a clock in this old room—is that what I saw doesn't make sense.

Two of the figures on the screen were average size, maybe a little short, but the child? Impossible. Even if someone managed to survive the elements, having a child is beyond the realm of insane.

It was one of the very few bright sides of Sam and Rhika's struggles with conception. They didn't have a little one to care for when everything went bad. Rhika confessed to me, once we'd finally made it to Colorado and gotten on the lottery list, that she didn't think we'd have made it if we had a child with us. We wouldn't have been able to do the things we had to do to survive.

I don't know if that was true, even then. But losing Nayaih was painful enough. I don't want to think about what it would have been like to lose Sam and Rhika's child.

I grit my teeth and push up from the cot. The blanket falls to the floor with a thump and a cloud of dust. I don't bother to pick it back up as I make my way to the open door.

I can't sleep with them closed anymore. Being in this mountain is claustrophobic enough.

My morning routine starts earlier than usual. When I hit the light on the wall of the Blue Box room, the clock shows it's barely 4am. I run a hand over my face, drawing the loose skin down as weariness permeates my bones.

I could go back to bed.

A shudder runs down my spine at the thought of going back to the cot, but a knotting in my gut stops me from heading toward the soft bed in the officer's quarters.

Instead, my gaze is drawn to the narrow hallway that leads to the little room of monitors. I could check. The cameras have a night vision mode. Even with the darkness outside...

No. There is no point in looking. I already know what I'll see. Nothing. My mind was playing tricks on me yesterday. That's all it was.

My fingers drift to the glass door of the Blue Box. It's tempting... so tempting to go again. To let this machine take me back to a time when the world wasn't broken.

I cross to the control panel against the far wall. A notepad sits there, its pencil worn down to the nub. My list of dates fluctuates. Some months it only shrinks as I cross off where I've gone. Sometimes I remember a new moment. A new date I can jump to.

The list has shrunk so much these past few weeks. It's what I get for jumping so many times in a row. Eventually I'll put in random dates. Days and times when I might not catch even a glimpse of Roger or the rest of them. I'll just be an old woman, sitting on a park bench and watching the ocean.

My hand curls into a fist as my throat constricts. The arthritis flares, and I relax my grip with a wince.

The room with the monitors calls to me again.

I leave the Blue Box and make for the mess hall. The room is the size of a gymnasium. My footsteps would echo if I were wearing shoes. My thick socks are quiet on the concrete floor.

The base is stocked to the gills. MRE packets line a hundred shelves, giant tubs of dried oats, cans of tomato sauce, and more. I've tried a little of everything, and barely made a dent in my twenty years within these walls.

I take my time this morning. I use dry milk, make myself something that resembles real oatmeal. There is no fresh fruit, no raisins or brown sugar or walnuts or honey to add to the grey mush. The process of making it is almost enough.

I clamber over a bench seat in the middle of the room. I don't know when it got so hard to make these simple movements, but my body aches and my movements are slow.

I eat. The sound of my own chewing is so loud in my ears.

My hands shake.

As my metal spoon hits the edge of the bowl and the sound echoes through the vast, empty room, my tears begin to fall.

Chapter Fifteen

Before

The first few houses are destroyed and, from all evidence, deserted. We pick through a few of them, nosing around in medicine cabinets and kitchen pantries to see if we can avoid going all the way into town.

Everything has been taken. Not a single canned good is left. Not even a moldy apple in a fruit bowl.

"If the rest of it looks like this..."

Sam grunts, on his hands and knees searching through the space under the kitchen sink. I check the garage, and then we move on.

This area was farmland. Acres of oat crops, withered and brown, surround us as we get closer to the town. We cross a little bridge over a half-frozen stream. The water froze so solidly during the last cold burst, there is still ice at the bottom.

Dead fish line the shore. Their stench clogs the back of my throat. I speed up, swallowing down the urge to retch.

The town of Fair Weather is small. It's clear when we've reached the main square. A classic small-town church sits at the end of the road, forming the head of a T intersection. The paint used to be white, and I'm sure the wooden cross at the top wasn't always missing a chunk of the right arm. It, like the rest of the buildings, has seen better days.

The silence around us is palpable. Tension sits in the air as our footsteps echo through the space. A barber shop, pharmacy, grocers, all quaint and old-timey to someone from a big city, appear deserted. However, as we move past a defunct concrete fountain with a chunk blown out of the bottom, I step closer to Sam.

"The doors are all closed," I murmur.

He nods. "Windows too."

We keep moving, aiming for the pharmacy as we go past a few vehicles parked on the sides of the road. A smaller green car has a hole in the roof. I lean down and spot a chunk of dented concrete underneath it.

"This town got hit hard by the ice."

Sam says nothing. He takes the rifle off his shoulder and holds it loosely against his arm. Casual, but ready.

A minute later, we are at the door to the pharmacy. The windows, clear glass, are boarded up on the inside with what looks like a combination of wood and cardboard. I grip the handle of the door. Sam stands to the side, gun in hand. With a nod, I pull it open.

The interior is dark. Light streams in through the doorway, casting a beam that goes across a corner of the check-out counter.

"Hello?" I call out in a tentative voice.

Sam widens his eyes at me.

"I don't want another gas station incident," I say. "If there's someone in here, I don't want to scare them."

"You don't have to worry about that," a voice says from the shadows.

Sam whirls, training his muzzle toward the darkness. As he does so, footsteps sound behind us and two figures step into the doorway, weapons in hand.

I put my hands up, heart thudding against my ribcage. "We don't want any trouble. We came to find medicine for a friend. That's all."

I step toward the counter as the men at the door move inside. One is tall, at least as tall as Sam. The other is only slightly shorter, but with a stockier build. It's impossible to make out clearer details with the only light behind them.

"Where did you come from?" the voice in the shadows asks.

I glance where I think the person might be. The voice is gravely and deep, but I can't tell if a man or woman is talking.

Sam's gaze darts to me and he gives a sharp jerk of the head, indicating that I refrain from answering. He follows my movement, stepping back as well to avoid the men from outside getting between the two of us.

"California," I reply, my voice steady. "We left before the tsunamis hit. Made it here, but our friend is very sick. We brought things to trade. For medicine."

There is a low laugh, and my nostrils flare as preemptive anger heats my belly.

I force a deep inhale, letting it out before asking, "What's funny?"

"Not so much funny as unexpected," the voice says. A form appears before us, almost materializing out of the darkness. "Get us some light, Jim. I can't see my damn hands, let alone our visitors."

There's a grunt from the shorter of the men before he walks toward one of the windows. After a moment of fiddling, a wooden panel folds down and a new beam of light illuminates the space and the people in it.

The voice belongs to an older woman, maybe in her fifties or sixties. Gray hair tumbles down around her broad face, the ends going just past thick shoulders wearing red flannel. Her right hand rests on the hilt of a machete clipped to her belt.

"What's unexpected?" I ask as she studies us and our supplies.

"That you'd come to trade, rather than to steal."

A frown furrows my brow. "Have other survivors looted the town?"

"Looted is a nice word for it. We were raided by a bunch of violent-minded men a week or so ago. They hurt some folks, ate through a lot of our stores before we finally chased them out of town."

"Aren't you worried they'll come back?" I ask, even as Sam nudges my arm with his elbow. A sign to stop asking so many questions.

"No."

"Why?" Another nudge.

"Because a few hours after they left, the ice came." She glances at the taller man, whose complexion turns a bit green. "Our people went down the road a ways to make sure they hadn't set up camp to wait and attack us at night. Turns out, that's exactly what they did. The ice..."

I glance out the door, toward the broken concrete fountain and the car with a hole in the roof.

"Well, we don't have to worry about them anymore."

Chapter Sixteen

Before

Vern, the older woman who runs what's left of the town of Fair Weather, gives us a little tour of the place. The people left, a few dozen of the 500 that used to be here, stay together for the most part. They sleep in the church, having fortified the roof with panels of metal and wood with hay as insulation.

Light shines through a few holes in the ceiling, but it appears their efforts kept the massive chunks of ice that fell not long ago from decimating everyone. The men who attacked them were not so lucky. Vern tells us even the supplies they stole didn't make it unscathed.

"It must have been a narrow storm," I say as we exit through the back of the church.

Most of the people we meet are near our age, a bit older. There aren't any children and Vern appears to be the oldest here. I don't want to ask where the young and elderly went. I'm sure I already know.

Sam still has his rifle at the ready, but Vern seems unconcerned. She walks a step ahead of me, leading the way to the barber shop where they are keeping medical supplies. Our escort has doubled, two men walk on either side of us.

Even if Sam got off a shot, we'd be taken down before he could shoot again.

I eye the machete at Vern's waist. One of those might come in handy.

"Why do you think so?" she asks, glancing at me.

"We got the frost, but no ice fell where we were. We heard it, though."

Behind me, Sam speaks up for the first time. "Sounded like a battalion marching to war. Like gunshots."

Vern nods. "We were lucky to have gotten the roof fortified before it hit. The cold caused some problems." She holds up her left hand, showing me the frostbitten tips of her pinky and ring finger. "A few others got it worse. We made the mistake of trying to keep watch at the door. Won't do that next time."

I nod, swallowing hard as I clench my hands into fists.

The weather today is mild, hovering in the 70s. It's almost enough to pretend the world is going to get back to normal. But the heat could come at any time. The cold.

Those we might be able to continue avoiding, but the other storms...

"Have you had any tornadoes?" I ask. "Any lightning storms?"

We reach the barber shop, and she pulls open the door for me, giving me a frown. "No. Why do you ask?"

"We caught a bit on the radio coming in," I say. "Storms all over the country, tornadoes in Canada, and the west coast is practically gone."

I look around, my gaze catching on Sam's glare just as I realize what I've said.

"Radio?" Vern raises an eyebrow. She scans my belt.

"Yeah," Sam growls, "a little hand-held one. The battery died, and we chucked it."

I nod, focusing on a neutral expression. "So," I rub my hands together and eye a red cooler on the counter, "what are you looking for in exchange for some Tylenol or Ibuprofen? Anything that will bring down a fever."

Vern hesitates, her gaze flitting between me and Sam with suspicion on her face. After a moment, she sighs. "We should have some Ibuprofen left. As far as an exchange, what do you have?"

Sam shoulders his rifle and digs through his pack. He pulls out a few of our heating packs and one flint set.

One of the men with us scoffs as Sam sets the things on the counter and takes a step back.

"That's it?"

I grit my teeth, heat flaring once again. I like Vern enough, but my nerves are too on edge to deal with anyone's sass.

"What did you have in mind?" I snap.

The man shrugs, a scowl on his face.

"Enough." Vern holds up a hand, giving her man a very parental look. She turns to me. "We don't have much left; this isn't enough for me to give up medicine."

Sam and I exchange a glance. My pack holds the same things his did, and we've already discussed not wanting to give up all of our supplies. This stuff might be all that stands between us and freezing to death.

"Would you take cash?" Sam asks.

At this, Vern chuckles. "No, young man. I will not take cash. Even when things get back to normal, it'll take a decade to get the banking systems up and running again."

Sam twists the wedding ring on his finger. It's silicone. A black band he got from Rhika to replace the silver one he lost hiking the PCT shortly after their wedding.

It has almost no monetary value.

But mine...

I swallow and slip the engagement ring from my finger. "What about this?"

Vern holds out a hand, and I drop the ring into her palm.

Chapter Seventeen

Now

Halfway through the day I can't keep myself away from the monitors any longer. The itching, nagging tick at the back of my mind won't stop. Like a gnat or a fly has entered my ear and keeps buzzing around.

I clean the parts of the bunker I use. A relatively small section considering the size of the mountain complex. I check the radio and my little morse code machine.

My attempts to read in the study are constantly interrupted by rushes of fear, of regret. I trick myself into thinking I see shapes, hear banging on distant doors. Eventually it's too much. I need to stare at the screen and see an empty street. I need to *see* the proof of my own mind having played a trick on me.

I stumble a bit on the way to the room. There are a few places where the floor isn't level; steps where I've found myself tripping every now and then. I curse and keep a hand on the wall the rest of the way.

My throat is dry as I push the door open. The chair is knocked to the side, leaning against one of the desks.

I grip the top of the plush fake leather with shaking, aching fingers and pull it upright. Deliberately avoiding the screen that lied to me before, I scan the others, check the satellites making their way over the ocean that used to be part of Europe.

My heart thuds against my chest. The sound of my own blood rushing through my ears makes me lightheaded. Finally, when the pressure has built too much to ignore, I turn my attention to the cameras outside the mountain.

Blank.

Empty.

Desolate.

I knew it. I stare, watching for movement. The wind blows a handful of leaves down the road. It looks nice outside. The temperature gauge says it's in the low 80s.

That could change in a matter of minutes.

There is no life. No rodents, no birds, and definitely no humans.

I shake my head, biting the inside of my lip and clenching the armrests of the chair. Foolish.

Tears blur the screen. I wipe them away, fury building in my gut until I slump forward and scream between my knees. The only way to let it out. To release the pain and anger and sadness in me.

When I sit up again, my heart nearly stops.

I blink, rub my eyes, and lean forward. A figure is walking up the road toward the door. A young man, by the build and the gait. He carries a pack on his back.

I lean closer, lips trembling as my fingers touch the screen. Another. A little shorter than the first but an adult frame nonetheless. The man reaches the door to the bunker and looks back. Behind them both...

My breath catches, a hand pressing to my throat. My eyes burn with tears not of anger, but some muddled combination of confusion and disbelief.

This one is a child. Absolutely a child.

But how?

My nose is half an inch from the screen. The tallest of the forms reaches up, makes eye contact with the camera, and waves.

I push back, heart hammering against my chest and eyes wide. A moment passes. Then another. The people outside settle in. They pull out blankets and sit, occasionally waving at the camera.

The little one laughs.

I bolt from my chair, run out of the room, and sprint down the hall as fast as my ancient legs will carry me.

Moments. Mere moments and everything could change.

The main level of the base is a twenty-minute walk from the section holding the Blue Box. The section I've made my home.

My footsteps reverberate through the long metal shaft that leads to the front door. The asphalt beneath my feet is as dark as the day it was poured, no sun to tarnish it to a dull grey.

The first door sticks when I punch in the code. Fear strikes my heart. I can't have forgotten. Can't have lost the numbers in my mind.

It's only time, time and age slowing the mechanisms the same way they slow me. The door grinds open, and I'm running again.

I hesitate at the last panel. Blood runs across my tongue from where my teeth have pierced the flesh of my lips. I hit the wrong number and have to wait a few seconds to try again.

Then it's done. The door is opening. Metal sliding against metal, grinding against concrete. Sun pours in, blinding me for a split second.

I hold up a hand, blocking the light as a voice echoes through the tunnel.

"Hello."

Chapter Eighteen

Before

Vern accepts my ring as payment for the medicine. Along with the supplies Sam leaves on the counter as we make our way out of town. No food. No water.

They had none to spare. Instead, we walk toward the jeep with two bottles of pills and an itch at the back of my neck.

"That went—"

"I'm sorry about your ring," Sam says. He glances at me, at the empty tan line where my engagement ring rested for so long.

I shake my head, brushing aside a lock of hair that escaped my braid. "I'm not. Roger will understand."

He nods. "Absolutely. Still, I wish we'd had something else to trade."

I spare a quick look behind us. The town slowly disappears from view, just the tops of the building visible now.

"I don't think we should stay here," I say, partially to change the subject, partially because it's very true. "I didn't mean to—" I grit my teeth. "I shouldn't have mentioned a radio."

Sam turns, walking backward a few steps with his gaze scanning the road and trees behind us. "You worried?"

"Always," I mutter.

He faces forward again and picks up the pace.

⚬

We get to the Jeep, and the back of my neck hasn't stopped prickling. Anxiety eats at my stomach, clawing at the inner line of my gut.

Sam hops into the driver's seat, but I hesitate with my hand on the passenger door.

I turn to look back the way we came. There's a crack like a whip, and a bullet whizzes past my ear and shatters the side mirror.

"Lu!" Sam shouts.

I duck, rushing around the back of the Jeep and kneeling on the soft dirt. Heavy breaths escape with little bursts of panic. Another shot rings out. Another shatter of glass as the windshield of the Jeep is hit.

Sam.

I loosen and drop the heavy pack on my back. Then I pull the rifle from my shoulder, check the safety, and cock it. Keeping low, I inch around to the driver's side of the trunk and peek my head out. Sam's door is open. His arm hangs out, blood dripping onto the road. Terror strikes through my heart.

"Sam," I hiss. Silence. "*Sam*." Louder this time.

His finger twitches. Not dead. Not yet.

"I'm sorry about this," an unfamiliar voice calls from down the road.

It's not Vern. My lip curls in a sneer. One of her lackeys. One of the ones who followed us around Fair Weather and wanted more than we had to give for the medicine.

"Not yet, but you will be," I shout back. My ears ring. Anger laces through me with every heartbeat.

"It doesn't have to be like that," says the man who just shot at me and my friend. "You can go. Leave the meds, leave the Jeep, and go back to wherever you came from."

"We made a fair trade," I holler. Ducking low, two pairs of feet are visible a good distance away, walking down the middle of the road toward us. "We had a deal."

"That was a shit deal," a new voice snarls. "Vern thinks the world will go back to normal someday. She's wrong. What you gave us ain't worth it. Not for those meds."

"Yeah." I can't keep the fury out of my voice. "It's all about the meds. That's why you're taking our Jeep too?"

Another glance shows that they've slowed.

My mind is pulled in a dozen directions. I need to stand, fire, kill them. Is Sam alive? Do they have a shot trained on him right now? Will they kill him if I move? The medicine. If we don't get it back to Nayaih she's going to die. The Jeep. They blew out the windshield, it won't work as a half-way decent shelter now.

With each thought comes a flash of anger.

The men don't respond to my question, and I'm done talking. I go back, curling around the side and returning to the busted mirror. They're looking to the driver's side. Looking at Sam.

The guns are limp, as though they think they're done fighting. As though the shots they took were enough to silence me.

I suck in a breath. My heartbeat slows. I tuck the butt of the rifle into my shoulder, and in a fluid movement rise, aim, and squeeze the trigger.

Chapter Nineteen

Before

The recoil sends me staggering back. I forgot to plant my feet. Still, I keep both hands on the weapon and bring it up, ready to fire again.

One of the men is down, blood pouring from his side. I shot him in the gut.

The other sprints toward the Jeep. I fire again, but the shot goes wide. I rush around, ducking as the man on the ground gets off a round. It hits the asphalt, flecks of black ripping through my pants and spraying into my shins.

The man reaches the driver's side, grabs Sam by the front of his jacket, and pulls him out. Sam yelps in pain. He's bleeding from the arm. His jacket hides the extent of the damage. A flesh-wound—I hope.

I raise the gun again, pointing at the man holding my friend. He's dropped his rifle, replaced it with a blade. Pressed to Sam's neck.

I freeze, one hand on the gun, the other rising in surrender. "Don't—"

Sam spins. With startling speed given his injury, he wheels and slams the man into the side of the Jeep.

The man grunts. He shoves Sam back, snarling and swipes with his knife. Sam jumps back, and my shot is clear.

My finger caresses the metal of the trigger. Blood sprays. The body, dead almost instantly, crashes into the side of the Jeep, my bullet buried in his heart.

Sam pants against the Jeep, clutching his shoulder. I rush forward.

"Are you—"

"I'm okay." He nods, grimacing and gives me half of a smile cut with a wince.

The heat in my chest rises to my face. Fury. Rage.

"What about the other one?" he asks, breaking me from the anger clouding my mind.

I turn and stalk back around the still open driver's side door. The man I shot moans on the ground, his gun forgotten beside him as he tries to hold the blood inside his body.

If he gets to help soon enough...

I march forward and kick his gun away just before he lunges for it. "That was a very stupid thing to do," I growl.

"Wait," his voice shakes, terror and pain lacing every word. "Please, I can explain."

"I don't need an explanation." Again, the steadiness of my words catches me off guard. Even my hands are calm, loosely gripping the weapon that just killed a man. At ease.

"No." He inches backward, tears pooling in his eyes. "We made a mistake. It won't... it wasn't..."

I watch him fumble with the words. The temperature here has remained the same, a mild day. But I feel ice. Cold in my gut replacing the heat of the short gun fight. A chill that seeps into my chest and finds a comfortable home in the ventricles of my heart.

"Lu," Sam calls from the Jeep.

I don't move my gaze from the man on the ground. "Yeah?"

"The people in town, they'll have heard the shots. We need to go."

I nod slowly. Realization grows like a storm in my mind. I think of Nayaih, the fever giving her skin a glassy sheen. Rhika, the expression I can picture on her face if I'd returned alone. Roger, the thought of something happening to the man I love.

I flip the safety on and hitch the rifle strap over my shoulder.

The bleeding man before me exhales a preemptive sigh of relief.

"Will the Jeep start?" I ask, loud enough for my voice to carry to my friend.

"Yeah, they blew out the windshield but missed the engine block."

I nod again, almost to myself this time. Solidifying what must be done in my mind. "I'll be right there."

There's a pause. Tension in the hesitation that sits on the air around me. I feel Sam's gaze. Feel the moment it clicks for him.

Feel when it clicks for the man on the ground.

"Wait," his voice is more frantic now. Fear seems to emanate from his very pores. "Please... I won't..."

"What?" I murmur, pulling the short knife from my belt and stepping forward.

He reaches out. I kick the hand away.

"Won't follow us?" I say. "Won't try to find us? Take what we have? Kill us?"

"Please, it was a mistake."

I nod, my face a stiff mask.

The man lets out a sob, his tears cleaning the grime from his face.

No more words.

I kneel, my knee touching down in the pool of blood around him. He's lost a lot already. Maybe he doesn't have a chance anyway.

I block out the sound of his pleas. He is weak, barely able to raise his hands to try and defend himself.

It takes more force than I expected to drive my blade into the side of his neck. Less to pull it out. It takes every ounce of will I have to watch the blood run. To watch his face pale, his eyes dim, his breathing stop.

When it's done, I wipe my blade clean on his pant leg. I take the machete off his belt, his gun off the ground, and then I hurry around the Jeep, scoop my bag from the back, and climb into the passenger's seat.

Sam doesn't speak, but I feel his gaze on me. When I don't return it, he shifts into drive, pulls off the shoulder, and takes us home.

Chapter Twenty

Now

A din of sounds assaults my ears. I wince, cracking my neck to the side and squeezing my eyes shut for a brief moment.

These children are loud.

Children. Indeed, all three of them are, though if memory serves the older ones won't like to be called so. I think the boy is in his early twenties. The girl, a bit younger, and the smallest is maybe six or seven.

The first place I take them is the mess hall. They don't sit, standing and awkwardly watching me as I slip into the massive pantry to gather some food. Each of them is thin, absurdly so. They remind me of those days after we lost Nayaih to the fever, trying to get somewhere safe. Finally making it to Colorado and camping out in front of the mountain, waiting on the lottery to get us in.

Before we found out that was all a bunch of bullshit. They only wanted people able to jump. Able to go back in time to try and fix the mess the world became.

I pull out the good stuff. Canned ravioli and green beans for the main course, peaches for dessert. They eat like ravenous wolves.

When the eating is done, the talking begins.

"We started at the coast," the boy says.

He's told me his name, but it's lost in the fog clouding my mind. It feels as though little crackles of lightning keep going off inside my head.

"The Appalachian Mountains," the older girl supplies, putting a hand on the little one's shoulder. "Our parents met at a shelter there. It was safe for a while. Tom and I kinda grew up there."

A flash of heat through my chest. How could anyone grow up in what the world has become?

"By the time Lu came along..."

The older two exchange a glance and fall silent. Lu, a little girl with knotted frizzy braids and wide brown eyes continues to stare at me, as she has since she finished her third can of peaches.

The silence permeates the mess hall, and my chest constricts. My throat is tight. I walk backward, keeping these people in my eyeline as I go for a bottle of water and down enough to settle my nerves.

Tom and the other one exchange another glance before standing and collecting the mess of dishes on the table.

Lu scrambles to help. One of the bowls falls, clangs to the ground with a sound that reverberates through the room.

I flinch, hand flying to the hilt of the blade at my waist.

Tom leaps forward, pushing Lu behind him and holding up a hand in a defensive gesture.

I dart a glance over my shoulder but see no sign of the danger he is protecting his sister from. Looking back at them, I note the girl—Grace, that was her name—clenching a metal fork in her hand. She stares at me with the same deep brown eyes as Lu.

Tom, too.

Staring at me.

I look down. My knuckles are white around the handle of my long dagger. I unclench my fingers and inhale a shaky breath.

"Not to worry," I murmur, my voice thick and hoarse. "Just a dish." I try for a smile, but the muscles in my cheeks don't remember the movement.

Lu clings to her brother's leg.

I take a few steps forward and reach down, plucking the bowl from the concrete floor and setting it on the stack of dishes still on the table.

Grace sets the fork down, her wary gaze still fixed on me.

"Why don't we take care of these later?" I say, keeping my voice as steady as I can. "I can show you a place to get some sleep."

It's hard to walk out of the room. Hard to put my back to them. My neck itches, the hair on my arms stands on end. My jaw aches from how hard I'm gritting my teeth.

Their footsteps are soft behind me. A murmured shuffle through the cavernous mountain. An echo of the ones who were here so long ago.

Chapter Twenty-One

Now

The children follow me like little ducklings. I don't know how to handle this. People, children, strangers in the bunker. My mind keeps flashing to the moments when I found Sam's body. Roger's. The man who killed them on the floor in the med bay, empty bottles of whisky and pills surrounding him.

I didn't even have the pleasure of getting revenge for my loved ones.

I snap out of the past as the children start talking. Their voices reach me, low whispers of sound designed to stay private. Hard to do in a place like this.

"...seems uneasy."

"Wouldn't you be?" Grace says. "How long do you think she's been in here?"

I clench my hands, fingernails digging into the flesh of my palms. "A long while," I mutter, my voice carrying to them a few paces down the hall. "We're here."

I say it, but as I step into the area of the bunker designed like a dorm with tiny cots, shared bathrooms, and flickering lights I'm hit with another flash of memories. Roger and I laughing together, finally feeling safe after so long in the elements. Pushing our two cots together and forgetting everything else for a precious few hours.

Those memories have been tainted and pushed down for so long, they surprise me. I put a hand on the door frame, glancing in at the room we shared. The children have gone ahead, poking their noses into other rooms down the hall.

My lips tremble.

"No."

Tom is the first to turn, watching me with wary eyes. "No?"

"No." I shake my head, clear my throat, and wave them toward me. "Sorry, not this section. There's..." I swallow. "There's a better area."

The siblings exchange worried looks that I see and choose to ignore. I avoided the officer's quarters because I sleep there. The thought of having them so near me...

But I can't let them sleep here.

"Come on." I make my way toward the nicer section of the mountain. My feet stumble every now and then, tripping on the uneven ground. I curse, purse my lips, and glance back.

The little one, Lu, is right behind me. Her curious eyes widen at my language but then her hands go over her mouth, and she lets out a string of giggles that echo around us.

I raise an eyebrow, my mouth twitching into an uneasy grin at how entertained she is by a few words.

"I'm not allowed to say that yet," she tells me. Behind her, the older two turn red. "But Grace and Tom can cuz they're old. You're old too so you can say whatever you want."

Mirth stirs in my stomach. A little balloon of a laugh makes it halfway up my chest before it deflates. I let out a brief chuckle, my smile stiff on my face.

"How much further?" Lu asks, oblivious to the fact that she elicited my first laugh in a decade. Her small hand scoops mine.

With a jerk, I pull away, heart racing and nerves shaking. Back to the wall, I focus on calm breaths. Tom stares. Grace takes the hand I abandoned and continues on with Lu.

"This way?" She turns back to glance at me.

I nod, still trembling. Trying not to keep my hand on my hilt because even though it would bring me a modicum of comfort, I know how it would look.

Tom waits a few paces away. Still watching me.

When I look at him, he shrugs and sticks his hands in his pockets. The movement is so like what Roger used to do anytime he felt uncomfortable, that another smile forces its way through my anxiety.

We make it to the officer's quarters. The doors are all open, unlocked, contents strewn about in some of them. I've taken something from every one of these rooms. A thick blanket from one, an ergonomic pillow from another, a set of those little round balls that click back and forth—I can't remember the name of them—and more.

The children don't notice anything missing. Tom raises an eyebrow at me as Lu bounces on the balls of her feet expectantly.

"Any room?"

I nod. "Mine is up the hall a ways," I say with a limp gesture. "These are up for grabs."

Lu squeals and races into the nearest one, Grace close behind. A few seconds later Lu's shouts and laughter boom through the concrete walls.

Grace steps back into the hall and rolls her eyes, but the grin suggests she's not annoyed in any form. "She's bouncing on the bed."

Tom's face breaks into a smile that seems to come easier than Grace's.

"Well." The word hangs in the air as the older children turn to look at me. I grit my teeth, a shudder going across my spine at the double set of eyes trained on me. I clear my throat. "I'm sure you're all tired. There are bathrooms in each room, but don't use too much water. A couple minutes, max."

Grace's jaw drops.

Tom steps toward me, eyes alight. "Water? Like, a shower?"

I give an affirmative jerk of my head. "Short."

He nods vigorously. "Yeah." Excitement shines on his face.

"I'll be around this evening," I say, feeling that bubble of amusement in my stomach again. "We can finish your tour then."

"There's more?" Grace asks, watching her brother hurry into the room Lu picked out.

"This bunker was designed to hold hundreds of people." I put a hand on the cold concrete wall, the words bringing a reminder of Sam's shouting matches with the soldiers in charge.

"How many..." Grace falters, her gaze roaming over the empty rooms until it lands on me. "Are you the only one here?"

There is no accusation in the tone, but I feel it just the same. The question under the question—*why?*

I clear my throat again. "Get some rest. I'll, uh... I'll get you all for dinner."

Grace gives a brief nod, her face breaking into a bemused smile as a shriek from the room suggests Tom showed Lu the shower.

Chapter Twenty-Two

Now

The next few days don't pass the way the last decade has—a blur of the same with no moments of recognition to distinguish between them. No, with Tom, Grace, and Lu here, there are plenty of moments to remember.

Tom's excitement over the shower is one. Lu finding my study and diving for the colored pencils is another. Then there's the day Grace finds the instruments. The same day I show them the Blue Box.

Most of the bunker is shut off. Powered down and closed so I don't waste heat and energy. But the children want a full tour, and I've been meaning to see if I can find a few things. So we move to the control room to turn the power on.

"Woah..." Tom's breathless murmur makes me hesitate as I reach for a set of switches.

I turn. The children stand before the large glass cylinder, eyes wide. Lu takes a few steps back, bumping into the control panel. Her chest rises and falls with quick, scared breaths.

"What is it?" Grace raises a hand, her delicate auburn fingers reaching toward the glass.

"Don't," I snap.

She drops her arm and faces me, lips downturned in a lightly hurt expression.

"It's..." I grimace. "It's dangerous."

Tom meets my eye. "It's a time travel machine."

Grace gives her brother a side-eye, and the corners of my mouth twitch up.

"That's not real," Grace says. "It's just a story." She goes to Lu and holds the little girl's hand.

Tom shakes his head. "It wasn't just a story until you got scared about it." He glances at the glass machine again. "Mom and Dad used to tell us about it. About the peo-ple—Futures?"

I give a grunt of confirmation, my breaths shallow.

"Futures who tried to fix the world before it broke. They—"

"Failed." I interrupt. "They failed."

Tom's eyebrows draw together, and he shakes his head. "Mom and Dad said they gave people time. Our parents only went to the mountains because the Futures said the world would flood. They only packed supplies that helped keep them alive because they knew what was coming. Dad, at least—" his face twitches here, the story he is telling becomes personal and a flash of pain twists his features, "—was grateful."

Grace stares at her brother. "I thought it was just a bedtime story."

He shrugs. "You got really freaked out when they were talking about it one time."

"Does it work?" Grace drops Lu's hand and steps toward the machine again.

"*Stop*," I say through gritted teeth.

She does as I say, though her eyes blaze with anger or frustration or annoyance.

"Why?"

I clench my jaw, another swarm of memories locking my tongue for a moment. The children wait, used to this after a few days of me learning how to speak to other humans again.

I inhale, my gaze drifting to my list. Only a few more days until it's safe for me to jump again. To see Roger, Sam, Nayaih, and Rhika.

Tears burn in my eyes. I blink them away and focus on Grace's dark gaze. Her smooth skin and corkscrew curls.

Rhika's hair looked like that after our first shower in the bunker. It had been years since a real shower for any of us.

She and Sam had gotten in trouble for going over the time limit.

"Not everyone can jump," I say. There's a tremor in my voice and, try as I might, I can't seem to steady it. "It takes a certain genetic make-up. If you don't have it, the machine..."

I can't. Not with Lu watching me with those wide, innocent eyes.

How? How are they still innocent with the world the way it is? How do they hold so much laughter when her parents are dead? Murdered by the men who chased them from their home. How is she able to smile after everything that has happened?

My cheeks are wet. The tears fell despite my protests.

Grace takes a tentative step forward and touches my forearm. I don't jerk away this time, but my hands still shake.

"What happened?" she murmurs.

Chapter Twenty-Three

Now

I tell them what happened to Rhika over lunch. I can't be in that room while I describe it. I can't look at the floor where Rhika's blood flowed. The glass cylinder that took weeks to scrub clean. The room of monitors where Sam barricaded himself with a blade.

It took eight hours for Roger and me to get him out. Eight hours at the door while the others cleaned the remains of one of our closest friends.

It took three months, and the threat of being kicked out of the bunker, for me to jump again.

"She wanted to help," I mutter, clenching my mug of minty water.

Tom has already taken a liking to my garden and refuses to drink plain water anymore. Every cup has mint, or cucumber slices, or lemon. It's a change that I didn't expect I'd enjoy.

"She couldn't stand doing nothing while I went, and she…" I choke on the emotion coursing through me. "She was almost a match. Off by two markers, they said. Close enough… and they were desperate enough to let her try."

Lu sits a few tables away, coloring with the bag of pencils she carries everywhere. Marks have shown up on the walls. Flowers and suns and other shapes I can't distinguish.

"She died," I say in a low voice, my gaze darting to Grace before looking down at my hands. I pick at my thumb nail. "The machine tore her apart."

We sit in silence for several long minutes. Tom's expression is grave, Grace's horrified.

"Could we get tested?" Tom asks. "To go back and try to fix things?"

The laugh that comes out of me isn't kind. It isn't funny. It's bitter and dark and sounds more like the real me. The me that kills, the me that lets people starve outside while my friends demand we do *something* to help, and I stay silent. The me that's lived alone for over a decade.

"There *is* no fixing things." I stare at Tom. "Time travel doesn't work the way they thought, the way they hoped. Everything I did had already been done. Do you understand?"

He shakes his head.

So I tell another story. The story of my engagement party. Of the old woman on the bench, the woman who was me. I'd already been there, already done the thing. Seen myself in the past and the present and the future and all that bullshit.

"There is no changing what already happened." There's a finality in my voice that carries through the room.

Grace and Tom exchange a glance, but they nod.

"Do you still go back?" Tom asks.

I give him a sharp look.

"I saw your list of dates."

My jaw clenches. "Yes. I still go back. But not to try and change things."

⸻ ◆ ⸻

It's a few hours later that Grace finds the Ukulele. The room is in the farthest end of the bunker, and my knees ache by the time we reach it. The children offered to go on their own. I refused.

Her face at the sight of the stringed instrument is worth the pain in my joints.

"You know how to play?" I can't keep the skepticism from my voice.

"Mom taught me." Grace clutches the little thing to her chest.

Shock, like a spark of electricity, hits my chest. Their community—though ruined now—once had people able to play and teach music.

What could *this* place have been?

"Look," Tom says, holding up a square package the size of his palm. "New strings too."

"Will you teach me?" Lu jumps up and down, poking her sister's arm.

Grace grins. "Absolutely."

We find other things. Items I passed over in my various searches of the mountain. Lu's eyes get so wide I worry they will burst when she finds a stack of unopened crayon boxes. They're in a closet I recall opening and closing years ago. There are some toys as well; stuffed animals sticky with dust, a porcelain doll, even a few of those little wind-up toys that hop around. Tom steps in front of the rest while Lu is focused on the crayons.

He gives me a wink and ushers Lu away. Later, while she's finding new and inventive names for the multitude of colors, he tells me he wants to save them for later. Presents for her next few birthdays.

I'm stunned into silence for the next few rooms the children scurry through.

Chapter Twenty-Four

Now

The next day Grace finishes re-stringing the instrument in my now crowded study.

Lu colors at the coffee table. We'll run out of paper at this rate. She's already covered most of the mess hall walls in her bright drawings.

Tom sits a cushion away on the same couch as me, thumbing through an encyclopedia and peppering me with questions every few minutes. The book I'm trying to get through, an old historical romance with not nearly enough romance, isn't as interesting as the moments his eyes light up, and he leans toward me with a new observation or query.

He was born after it all. After the world I grew up in had ended.

I tell him about cars. Trucks, planes, trains, and the other multitude of moving machines that carried us all from one place or another. He's fascinated by trade routes. The idea of massive crate ships bringing food, toys, tools, and parts across the vast ocean entertains him enough that I fully extinguish my limited knowledge of the subject.

Grace plucks at her Ukulele, reminding her fingers how to move and re-forming the calluses she had before they fled the Appalachian Mountains.

I glance at the clock on the wall. Evening approaches, and I plan on going to bed early. I'm able to jump tomorrow, it's been a full two weeks now. Long enough that I shouldn't suffer too many consequences from going.

I'll leave later in the morning this time, so I return after these three have gone to bed. They don't need to see me retching into a bucket, shaking from limb to limb. And I'll need some space to recuperate my emotions.

We have dinner. It's strange, having people here while I eat. Having someone standing next to me at the counter mixing hot water with a bag of freeze-dried pasta. Tom keeps talking—I don't know if he's ever going to stop again. Going on about the garden. Plans to expand, to find more solar lights and start saving some of the vegetables to use their seeds. He chops up squash and tomatoes to thicken the sauce.

I don't know when I lost interest in making food taste good. Eating has been for survival, not enjoyment, for so long...

Lu asks for more peaches after her second can. Tom tells her no, says we need to save them for later. Says we need to make sure we have some for special days.

After, while Tom and Lu clean up the dishes, Grace plunks down on the top of the table and strums a few chords.

I'm nibbling on a very stale cookie—fished out of the deep freezer by Grace yesterday—listening absent-mindedly. The tune is familiar, in that way that a smell from your childhood is familiar. It sends pins and needles across my skin.

Then she begins to sing.

My breath catches and the cookie falls onto the table. The song is *San Francisco*, by Ingrid Michaelson. It was Nayaih's favorite for rainy days—the very few we had. It was her sad song. The one she made me listen to on repeat when life was throwing nonstop pain our way. That was before. When we thought break-ups and getting fired and losing apartments were the worst things that could happen.

We'd sit at the park across from the Golden Gate bridge, sharing earbuds and watching the fog burn off the bay.

I breathe, the tears in my eyes cascade down my cheeks, catching in the wrinkles of my skin.

Grace's voice fades, humming along with the end of the song as I double over with the weight of emotion. A dam bursts within and the tears won't stop. Sobs come next. Gasping, shoulders shaking as years of pain and loss and loneliness erupt from me.

I'm too lost in it to flinch when a hand touches on my shoulder. Another, smaller one rests on my arm.

Lu leans her forehead against me. The warmth is so foreign. So far from my reality.

I shift, letting my head rest against her soft curls.

⸺◆⸺

The next morning, we are in the study. I'm back to my usual self, and it's easy to pretend my meltdown didn't happen. Easy-ish.

Grace gives me a hesitant look before she reaches for the Ukulele. Tom, mid-way through asking a complicated question, pauses. I give the girl half a nod and a stiff smile.

To my relief, she picks a different song to practice. One from a thin book she found on a bottom shelf. I make a point to ask where she learned *San Francisco*. To ask if she understands the words without the context of knowing anything about the city, or the world it was written in.

But not today.

Today Tom and I pore over a set of maps. He wants to rewrite them. Fix them to reflect the new lines of the world. What we know of them, at least.

We get through a few sketches with pencil, and he glances up at the clock.

"Are you still jumping today?"

I follow his gaze. It's well into mid-morning and we've barely started.

Lu looks at the clock too. "Why are we looking at the circle on the wall?"

My lips slant up into a smile, a crooked thing I don't recognize in the mirror. There is so much to teach her. To teach all of them.

Grace pauses her plucking and looks at me expectantly.

I meet her eye for a brief moment before turning back to Tom and the map. "Maybe tomorrow."

Epilogue

Now

It's been three years since I last jumped.

I had to go back, one last time, to say goodbye. I sat on the bench, the one Nayiah and I used to frequent. I watched the fog burn off the bay.

Three years have gone by with Tom and Grace and Lu, watching them learn and grow in the safety of the mountain. We've celebrated birthdays, crafted inventions, and mapped out every inch of the remaining world with the help of the satellites still in orbit.

The flavors and excitements of life, which had left me so completely, returned a little at a time with each moment of joy the children experienced.

It took hours of convincing, countless promises, and Lu's big, bright-eyed pleading, but the day has come.

I stretch my aching limbs in front of the monitors. No movement from outside. No freezes for months, no storms.

No people.

But they're out there. Somewhere, in the world, are survivors. People like Tom, ready to rebuild a community. People like Grace, wanting to bring music back. People like Lu, filled to the brim with hope.

"Are you sure you're ready?" Grace's gentle voice, still cautious around me after the stories I've told, sounds from behind me.

I turn from the screens, my smile steady. "I am."

Tom comes to her side. His jawline is shadowed with dark scruff. It's coming in faster and faster these days. "It's alright if you want to wait," he murmurs. "We don't mind."

"We don't want to rush you." Lu enters as well, causing the little room to become cramped. She's grown as well. The top of her head, hair braided into a pattern of swirls, almost reaches my chin.

My nose itches. Tears burn, unfallen, in my eyes as I look upon this new generation of hope. These people who saved me.

"I'm ready," I say.

We walk in silence. Footsteps echo around us, and I vividly recall my hurried movements years ago. My fingers, tight with arthritis, punch in the code.

Before us, the massive concrete door grinds against the ground, and sunlight pours into the mountain.

It bathes us all in warmth. Instead of flinching away, I close my eyes and tilt my face toward the heat. It feels different somehow. As though it's the world that changed, not me.

Tom tightens the holster on his belt, then rests his hand on the hilt of the machete I gave him. Grace adjusts the straps on her backpack, and Lu does the same with a wide grin at her sister.

I grip the walking stick the children insist I use. The bag on my back is light. We aren't leaving for good. Just a stroll. An exploration.

Maybe we'll find survivors. Maybe we'll find adventure.

I take Lu's outstretched hand. I hear Grace's excited exhale. I meet Tom's eye.

With a nod, we step into the world.

Acknowledgements

To the family I've found along the way. I cannot express my appreciation for you. I love what we are building, and I wouldn't trade a single moment if it meant losing the paths that led to you all and the lessons I've learned to get here.

9 781960 659255